HOCUS POCUS

HOCUS POCUS

A novel by Todd Strasser
Based on the motion picture from Walt Disney Pictures
Executive Producer Ralph Winter
Based on the screenplay by Mick Garris and Neil Cuthbert
From a story by David Kirschner and Mick Garris
Produced by David Kirschner and Steven Haft
Directed by Kenny Ortega

Disney
PRESS
NEW YORK

About the Author

Todd Strasser has written many award-winning novels for young and teenage readers. He speaks frequently at schools about the craft of writing and conducts writing workshops for young people. He and his wife and children live in Westchester County, New York. They don't light candles on Halloween.

To Emily and Adam Wickersham

Prologue

Salem, Massachusetts
October 31, 1693

IN THE DIM LIGHT before dawn, a door creaked somewhere in the house where fifteen-year-old Thackery Binx and his family slept. Thackery's eyes burst open as the faint sound of cackling laughter floated in through the window. He turned and looked at the small wooden bed where his seven-year-old sister, Emily, slept.

The bed was empty.

Thackery instantly sensed that something was wrong. Emily never liked to get out of bed on cold fall mornings. Besides, her dress and underclothes were still hanging by the hearth. She wouldn't have gone outside in her bedclothes.

Thackery quickly got up. He had reason to be concerned. The day before, Emily had eaten a candy crow, and since then she'd behaved oddly, as if she was in a daze. Thackery sometimes found his little sister annoying, but just the same he was worried about her.

Pushing open the front door, Thackery looked outside. The sky was gray, and the air was cool and moist. The grass was covered with a silvery film of dew. Suddenly he saw a sight that sent a shiver deep through him. Emily, wearing a nightgown and a sleeping cap, was following a caped figure up the hill toward the house where the three Sanderson sisters lived.

"Emily!" Thackery shouted, and started to run after her. He'd heard rumors about the Sanderson sisters. Some people claimed they'd heard strange chants coming from within the house. Others insisted they'd heard children's screams.

It was even whispered that the three reclusive sisters might be witches.

"Emily, stop!" Thackery cried, but neither his sister nor the caped figure looked back. As he ran after them, Thackery now saw another chilling sight. Strange purple smoke started to twist and curl from the chimney of the Sandersons' house. Thackery feared it could mean only one thing—that inside a spell was being cast.

He raced through the woods and underbrush. Branches and thorns tore at his nightshirt, but he didn't dare slow down. As he drew closer to the house, he saw Emily being beckoned inside by a bent, hooded figure wearing a blood red cape. Then the door slammed shut behind them.

A waterwheel turned and splashed beside the house. The purple smoke rising from the chimney now took the shape of demons and beasts. As Thackery scrambled closer, his heart began to beat hard with terror, but he knew there was no time to turn back and get help.

He reached the house and peered through a small window into a large room lit by candles. A black cauldron hung boiling in the fireplace, and many rows of small glass bottles lined the walls. In the center of the room, three old hags dressed in black huddled around Emily.

Thackery gasped and stepped back from the window. Suddenly an old nail on the waterwheel caught his nightshirt and lifted him into the air. Scared almost witless, Thackery flailed silently as he rose higher and higher. Then his eyes found the sloping roof of the house and he grabbed it, pulling his nightshirt free.

Moments later Thackery climbed through an open window on the second floor and crawled onto a loft overlooking the large candlelit room. He saw that two of the old hags had moved closer to the cauldron, and one of them was reading from a thick book. The third hag held Emily, who was strangely still. Watching her,

Thackery felt his stomach churn with helpless fear.

"Ah, here it is!" the hag with the book cackled, pointing at a page with one of her bony fingers. "The life potion."

While she read the recipe, the other witch added the necessary ingredients—a dead man's toe, some newt saliva, several drops of poison ivy. Thackery watched in stunned amazement. Any doubts he'd had about the Sanderson sisters being witches now vanished.

"One final item, and all is done," said the witch with the book. " 'Add a piece of thine own tongue.' "

Without hesitation she bit down on her tongue. Blood spurted from her mouth, and she spit the piece of tongue into the cauldron. Frozen with fear, Thackery watched the bubbling brew inside suddenly foam and change colors.

" 'Tis ready!" the witch cried with delight, dipping a wooden spoon into the cauldron and then offering it to Thackery's sister. "One drop of this and her life will be ours."

Before Thackery could react, Emily swallowed the potion. Thackery's eyes went wide.

"Nooooo!" he shouted, and jumped down from the loft, knocking over the boiling cauldron.

"A boy!" one of the witches cried.

Thackery ran to Emily, but before he could reach

her, the witch with the book aimed her gnarled fingers at him.

Zaaaapppp! A mysterious force struck Thackery and knocked him to the floor, leaving him stunned. Meanwhile, the witches turned back to Emily, who had begun to glow.

" 'Tis her life-force," one of the witches said. "The potion worked! Take my hands, dear Sisters. We shall share her."

As Thackery watched helplessly from the floor, the witches drew close to one another and inhaled. The glowing light left Emily in three streams, each stream entering one witch's mouth. Thackery gasped as Emily's golden hair turned thin and gray and her skin wrinkled. At the same time, the witches began to grow younger. One pulled back her hooded cape to reveal long golden locks of hair.

"I am beautiful!" she cried in delight. "Boys will love me."

The others also turned younger, but not enough to satisfy themselves.

"I will be younger still," muttered the one with red hair as she stared at herself in a mirror, "once I've sucked the life out of all the children in Salem!"

All the children? The thought released Thackery from his daze.

"Hag!" he shouted angrily at the red-haired witch.

"There are not enough children in the world to make *thee* young and beautiful!"

The red-haired witch spun and fixed a steely glare on him. "Hag, did you say? You will pay for that insult!" She snapped her fingers, and Thackery watched in amazement as her spell book flew across the room to her. It opened by itself and flipped through its own pages.

"Aha!" The red-haired witch smiled cruelly. "Your punishment will not be to die, but to live forever with the guilt of not being able to save your sister."

She began to chant:

> Twist the bones and bend the back.
> Trim him of his baby fat.
> Give him fur, as black as black.
> Just like this, he is a cat!

Salem, Massachusetts
October 31, 1993

"ONLY MOMENTS AFTER Winifred Sanderson turned Thackery Binx into a black cat," Ms. Olin told the sophomores in the darkened classroom, "the front door of the house crashed down, and villagers carrying pitchforks and wooden crosses rushed in and took the witches prisoner."

At his desk halfway down the third aisle, fifteen-year-old Max Dennison rested his chin in his hand. He couldn't believe his teacher had turned off the lights to tell this dumb ghost story.

"Later, the Sanderson sisters were hanged by the Salem townsfolk," Ms. Olin said. "But not before Winifred Sanderson promised that one Halloween when the moon was full, she and her sisters would be brought back to life and would steal the lives of all the children in Salem."

Who cares? Max thought miserably. He still couldn't believe that his parents had decided to move to Salem from California. They said they did it for his sister, Dani, and him, but who were they kidding? If his parents really cared about them, why did they drag them three thousand miles away from all their friends?

"And there are those who say that on Halloween night a black cat still guards the old Sanderson house," Ms. Olin went on, "warning off anyone who might bring the witches back to life."

An eerie silence descended over the classroom as the kids took in the story.

"Booo!" Ms. Olin suddenly shouted.

"Ahhh!" Half the kids in the room screamed.

"Scared you!" Ms. Olin laughed and flicked on the lights. "Works every year."

Max looked around at his breathless classmates and rolled his eyes in disbelief. "Give me a break," he muttered.

Suddenly Ms. Olin turned and stared at him. "So, we have a skeptic in our midst," she said with a smile. "Mr. Dennison, perhaps you'd like to share your fresh California point of view with us."

Max felt the eyes of the entire class on him. He turned and gazed across the aisle at Allison, an incred-

8

ibly pretty girl with long light brown hair and a slim turned-up nose. Max gave her a slight smile and turned back to Ms. Olin.

"Okay," he said. "Granted, you guys in Salem are all into black cats and witches and stuff. But everyone knows Halloween was invented by the candy companies. It's just a conspiracy to sell more candy!"

Max grinned, quite pleased with his explanation. But the rest of the class just stared blankly at him. Max felt his grin evaporate.

Suddenly Allison cleared her throat.

"It just so happens that Halloween is based on the ancient feast called All Hallows' Eve," she said. "According to the legend, it's the one night of the year when the spirits of the dead can return to walk among the living."

Max had a sudden idea and quickly jotted his phone number in his notebook. He tore out the page and handed it to her. "Well, if Jimi Hendrix turns up tonight, here's my phone number."

Briinnngg! The school bell rang, and kids started to gather their things together.

"Happy Halloween!" Ms. Olin called. Max picked up his books. He hoped to talk to Allison, but she raced out of the room ahead of him.

"Oh, Max," Ms. Olin said as he walked toward the door.

"Yes?" Max stopped.

"When you see Mr. Hendrix, please tell him I said hello." Ms. Olin winked at him. Max gave her a look as if she were crazy, and left.

It wasn't easy being a new kid at school—especially a new kid who'd started almost two months late. At the end of the day, Max stepped out of the building and looked around at the groups of kids talking excitedly about their Halloween plans. Max had no plans. He stood for a moment at the top of the steps, gazing at the brilliant orange, red, and yellow leaves on the trees.

Suddenly Allison passed by him. She was wearing a black cape and carrying a large ceramic bowl.

"Hey, Allison!" Max hurried down the steps to catch up to her. Allison stopped and turned to him.

"Oh, it's you," she said.

"Look," Max said. "I didn't mean to shoot you down before."

"You didn't?" Allison studied him without expression. It was hard for Max to know what she was thinking. He figured he had better say something nice.

"So, uh, that's a nice bowl," he said.

"Thank you. I made it in pottery shop."

"Uh, my name's Max Dennison."

"I know," said Allison. "You just moved here from California."

"Last week," Max said.

"Salem must be a big change for you," Allison said.

"That's for sure."

"You don't like it here?"

"Well, the leaves are nice," Max said. "But all this witch stuff. . . ." He shook his head.

"You don't believe in it?" Allison smiled mysteriously.

"Stuff like the Sanderson sisters?" Max shook his head. "No way."

The smile on Allison's face grew a little bigger. "Not even on Halloween?"

"Especially not on Halloween," Max said.

Allison reached into her pocket and handed Max a folded piece of paper. "Trick or treat," she said, and walked away.

Max unfolded the paper. It was the note with his phone number that he'd given Allison in class. Boy, I really blew that, he thought.

Max got his bike and started to ride home. He was really depressed. He missed his old friends, and now he'd just blown his chance with Allison. As he rode past the old graveyard, he didn't even notice the two guys on the sidewalk ahead.

"Halt!" one of them said, lifting his hand.

Max looked up and hit the brakes. He felt a shiver as he saw who had stopped him. One guy was scrawny, with long, greasy blond hair that fell over his shoulders. The other was bigger and wore an eight-ball jacket. His hair was cut short. Just that day Max had seen them both sitting outside the principal's office on suspension.

"Who are you?" the scrawny kid asked.

"Max. I just moved here."

"From where?"

"Los Angeles," Max said nervously, wishing he'd taken another route home.

"Dude!" the scrawny kid said mockingly.

"Tubular!" said the big guy, with a nasty grin.

"I'm Jay," said the scrawny kid. "And this is Ernie."

Ernie punched Jay hard in the arm. "How many times I gotta tell you my name ain't Ernie no more? It's Ice."

Ernie turned his head around, and Max saw that *ICE* had been shaved into his hair.

"Correction," Jay said, rubbing the sore spot on his arm. "This is Ice."

"Nice to meet you," Max lied. He started to go past them, but Jay blocked his way.

"Let's have a butt," he said.

"I don't smoke," Max said.

"They're very health conscious in L.A.," Ernie said with a smirk.

"How about some cash?" Jay said, holding out his hand. "You got any money on you, Hollywood?"

Max shook his head. Ernie looked disappointed.

"Jeez, no smokes and no money," he said. "What am I supposed to do with my afternoon?"

"You could learn to walk without scraping your knuckles," Max suggested.

It probably wasn't the best thing to say. Jay frowned angrily and stared down at Max's new sneakers. His frown became a grin.

"Whoa, new cross-trainers," he said.

"Cool, let me try 'em on," said Ernie.

"Uh, later, guys," Max said quickly, and tried to ride away. But Jay grabbed the handlebars of his bike and stopped him.

"Hey, Hollywood, didn't you hear what Ice said?" he asked. "He wants to try the shoes, *dude.*"

A little while later Max rode down the street toward his new house. It was actually an old ship captain's house, with a view of the bay. His parents planned to restore it in their spare time.

Max parked his bike and padded in his socks through the front door. In the living room his parents were unpacking boxes from the move.

"Hi, Max, how was school?" his mother asked in a cheerful voice.

"It sucked," Max muttered.

"Hey! Language!" Mr. Dennison said sternly.

"I can't believe you made me move here." Max glared at them.

His parents gave each other a glance, then looked back at Max.

"What happened to your shoes?" his mother asked.

"Don't ask." Max turned to the stairs and climbed them two at a time.

He had to go up two flights of stairs to get to his room, which was at the top of the house. Outside his door were signs that said Max Only! and Keep Out! At least Max had gotten his room the way he liked it. It was a mess. Clothes, CDs, and magazines were all over the place. Max went to his desk, pulled out a bag of chocolate-chip cookies, and sat down on his bed.

What a miserable day, he thought as he ate a cookie. He didn't know anyone at school. Those mutants Jay and Ernie had taken his new sneakers, and he'd made a fool of himself with Allison.

Allison . . .

Just the thought of her filled Max with yearning. If only he could touch her long brown hair. If only he could hold her in his arms . . .

Max put down the bag of cookies and picked up his pillow.

"Oh, Allison," he said, softly caressing his pillow. "You're so soft and beautiful."

Suddenly his closet door swung open, and his seven-year-old sister, Dani, leapt out. She had straight black hair and was wearing chicken-bone earrings, pointy glasses, and a ratty old fur stole.

"Ah-ha-ha-ha-haaaa . . . ," she cackled like a witch, then pointed a finger at him. "I scared you! I scared you!"

Max rolled his eyes. Dani was the biggest pain in the world. "Why are you dressed like that?"

"I'm a witch," Dani said, climbing onto his bed. She pressed her face close to his and puckered her lips. "Kiss me, I'm Allison."

"Drop dead." Max turned away.

"Don't be such a crab," Dani said, taking a cookie from the bag. "Guess what? You're taking me trick-or-treating."

"No way." Max shook his head. The last thing he wanted to do was have everyone see him taking his little sister around.

"Mom says you have to."

"Let her take you," Max said.

"She can't. She and Dad are going to a party at the town hall."

"Then go trick-or-treating by yourself," Max said. "You're old enough."

"I can't," Dani said. "I've never done it here before. I'll get lost. Besides, it's a full moon tonight. The lunatics will be out."

Max rolled his eyes and pulled the bag of cookies

away from her. Dani came close again and put her arm around his shoulder.

"Come on, Max," she said. "Can't you forget about being a cool teenager for one night? We used to have so much fun trick-or-treating together. It'll be like old times."

"Forget it, Dani. The old days are dead."

The corners of Dani's mouth turned down, and she jumped off the bed. "I don't care what you say!" she yelled angrily. "You're taking me!"

Bang! Dani ran out of the room and slammed the door behind her. Max shook his head wearily. Why couldn't they have left her back in California?

About twenty minutes later there was a knock on Max's door, and Mr. Dennison poked his head in. "Come on, Max," he said solemnly. "Let's take a walk."

Max knew he was in trouble. He followed his father down the stairs, out of the house, and down to the bay. Hundreds of sailboats and cabin cruisers were moored in the harbor. Max picked up a flat stone and skimmed it over the water. Mr. Dennison started his lecture.

"We moved here so that you and Dani could live in a safe, clean environment," he said.

"If it's so safe and clean, why can't Dani go trick-or-treating by herself?" Max asked.

"Because she's only seven years old, Max."

"Well, I'm sixteen," Max said, skimming another rock. "Nobody my age goes trick-or-treating."

"First of all, you're fifteen," his father said. "Second, Dani's really counting on you. Why don't you bring a friend along?"

"Because all my friends are in California."

"What about this girl Allison?" Mr. Dennison asked. "I hear you're crazy about her."

Max stared at him in shock. Then he looked back at the house. He clenched his fists and wished he could kill his little sister. "I can't believe she told you! She blabs her fat mouth, and then you expect me to take her trick-or-treating? Forget it. No way. Now it's totally out of the question."

Max's father crossed his arms. "Well then, I guess getting your learner's permit is out of the question, too."

Max felt his jaw drop. "That's unfair. Totally unfair!"

"Hey, I never told you life was fair," his father said. "Now suit up."

"What are you talking about?" Max gasped.

"Dani wants you to wear a costume."

Talk about adding insult to injury! Max stared at his father. "You're kidding, right?"

"Nope." Mr. Dennison started back toward the

house. "And don't do anything to scare her, Max. She'll get nightmares."

"Great!" Max shouted at him. "She just *gets* nightmares. I'm *living* one."

Max spent the rest of the afternoon in his room listening to Ozzy Osbourne and Megadeth. As soon as it started to get dark, he looked out his window and saw groups of costumed little kids being led from house to house by their parents. It was totally humiliating to think that soon he and Dani would be joining them.

"Come on, Max," he heard his father call from downstairs. "It's time to go."

Max put on sunglasses and a baseball cap and went downstairs. Maybe he was going trick-or-treating, but he *wasn't* going in costume. Inside the front door, his mother was putting bright red lipstick on Dani's lips. Max's sister was now wearing an orange-and-black witch's costume with the traditional pointy black hat.

"Can't you look happy?" Mr. Dennison asked him.

"No," Max replied.

His father frowned. "What are you supposed to be, anyway?"

"A rap singer," Max said.

"Shouldn't you wear the hat sideways?"

"No."

Mrs. Dennison opened the front door. Dani picked up a candy sack and hurried out.

"Have fun!" her mother called. "Watch out for cars!"

Max paused in the doorway, dreading what would come next. His father put a hand on Max's shoulder.

"Go on," Mr. Dennison said, gently pushing him out. "And don't forget what we talked about."

It's blackmail, Max thought as he stepped outside. Suddenly he looked up and noticed the full moon. He wasn't sure he'd ever seen it look so big and bright before. He tried to remember what Ms. Olin had said. If the moon was full on Halloween, those witch sisters could come back. He shook his head. What a bunch of rubbish.

"Coming?" Dani asked.

"Yeah." Max joined Dani on the sidewalk. They started down the street. Max had to admit that he'd never seen pumpkins so ornately carved. Some houses even had mechanical skeletons and ghosts that sat up and waved.

"Isn't this great?" Dani gushed.

"No," Max said, looking around furtively.

"Why are you looking around like that?" Dani asked.

"I'm worried someone will recognize me," Max said.

"If you'd worn a real costume, nobody would recognize you," Dani said. "Hey, want to try that house?" She pointed at an old gray house near a bus stop. On its porch a dozen jack-o'-lanterns flickered.

"Why not?" Max said with a shrug.

As they went up the walk, Dani pulled a second candy sack out of the one she was carrying and handed it to Max. "Here."

"Forget it," Max said. "I don't want any candy."

"That's what you say now," Dani said as she rang the doorbell. "But when we get home you'll start eating all my good stuff."

"Oh, all right." Max took the sack.

The door swung open, and an older man dressed in black with horns and a tail stood before them. Weird horror movie music was playing in the background.

"Abandon all hope, ye who ring my doorbell!" the man cried.

Max rolled his eyes. "I guess you're supposed to be the Devil."

"Trick or treat," said Dani.

The Devil rubbed his hands together. "Well, well, what have we here? A little witch and a kid wearing sunglasses."

"I'm a psychotic teenager," Max said.

The Devil gave them candy, and they continued to

the next house. Before long their candy sacks started to get heavy, but Max was still bummed out.

"Can't you lighten up, Max?" Dani asked as they worked their way down another block.

"You want me to lighten up?" Max asked. "Let's go home."

"Not yet," Dani said.

They turned a corner. Up ahead a bunch of kids were gathered under a streetlight, smoking and talking. Max suddenly froze. He'd just recognized Jay and Ernie.

"UH, LET'S GO THIS WAY," Max said, quickly turning in the opposite direction. But Dani kept walking right toward the crowd.

"Ding-ding," Ernie said, putting his arm down like a toll gate.

"Gotta stop and pay the toll, kid," said Jay.

"Ten chocolate bars," Ernie added. "And no licorice!"

"Just dump out your sack," Jay said. "We'll pick what we want."

"Drop dead, moron," Dani snapped.

Ernie stepped closer to her. "Yo, twerp. How'd you like to get hung off that telephone pole?"

"I'd like to see you try," Dani dared him. "Because it just so happens that I've got my big brother with me. Max!"

She turned and waved at him. Max couldn't believe what Dani had gotten him into. As he came closer, he saw that Ernie was wearing his cross-trainers.

"Hey, it's Hollywood!" Ernie said.

"Doin' a little trick-or-treating?" Jay asked with a grin. The other guys in the crowd laughed.

"I'm just taking my little sister around," Max said, feeling mortified. "That is, if it's okay with you."

"Protecting your baby sister." Jay smirked. "Aw, that's nice. And I just love your costume. Are you supposed to be a New Kid on the Block?"

The other guys laughed again. Dani put her hands on her hips and glared at Jay.

"For your information," she said, "he's supposed to be a Little Leaguer!"

Now the guys really cracked up. Max wished he could disappear. He took Dani's arm and started to lead her away.

"Uh, later, guys," he said to Jay and Ernie.

"Wait a minute," Ernie said. "Everyone pays a toll."

"Stuff it, zitface," Dani snapped.

"Why, you little—" Ernie reached out to grab her.

"Max!" Dani cried.

"Hey!" Max had no choice but to jump between them. Ernie pressed his oily face right into Max's and

23

clenched his fists. Max knew he was going to get creamed if he didn't think of something fast.

"Here, Ice," Max said, dropping his candy sack at Ernie's feet. "Have fun pigging out."

Ernie went for the sack, and Max quickly turned Dani around. As he led her away, Ernie called out behind them. "Hey, Hollywood! The shoes fit great!"

The crowd of guys laughed. Max and Dani walked back down the sidewalk. Max felt awful.

"You should have punched him," Dani muttered.

Max couldn't believe it. "He would have killed me!"

"At least you would have died like a man," Dani said.

That hurt. "Hey," Max said angrily. "You just humiliated me in front of half the guys at school. Go collect your candy and get out of my life!"

Dani scrunched her face up. "I want to go home now!" she shouted. She ran a little way down the sidewalk and then sat on some grass and started to cry. Now Max really felt bad. Even though Dani was a pain, she was just a little kid. Max knew he was all she had right now. Besides, if Dani told their father, Max would probably never get his learner's permit. He walked over and sat down next to her.

"Come on, Dani," he said, trying to be nice.

"Shut up!" she shouted. "I hate you! You've ruined everything. You ruined Halloween, and it was my

24

favorite time of the year except for Christmas and my birthday."

"Hey, I'm sorry," Max said. "It's just that I hate Salem. I miss my friends. I want to go back home, to California."

"This is your home now," Dani said with a sniff. "You might as well get used to it."

Max took a deep breath and sighed. He knew Dani was right. "Yeah, yeah. How about giving me one more chance, okay?"

"Why should I?" Dani sniffed.

"Because I'm your brother," Max said.

Dani shrugged and looked away. Max knew he had to get her back into the Halloween spirit or else wait until he was seventeen to learn to drive. He pointed at the full moon.

"Hey, look! Did you see that?"

"What?" Dani quickly looked up.

"Something just flew across the moon!" Max said.

As Dani squinted upward, Max reached around her and tickled her ribs.

"Ahh!" Dani jumped up. Breathing hard, she stared at her brother.

"Fooled you." Max grinned.

"Very funny." Dani crinkled her nose at him. "Let's go, jerkface."

They started down a street lined with old-fashioned

gas streetlights. The houses here were the biggest Max had seen in Salem. He stopped in front of one mansion that had tall white columns in front. He'd never seen anything like it in California.

"Wow," Max gasped. "Look at this house!"

The front door was open, and through it they could hear the sounds of laughter and talking.

"Rich people." Dani sounded disgusted. "They'll probably make us drink cider and bob for apples."

"Come on, let's check it out," Max said.

They went up the front walk and stepped into the house. The entryway was lit with glowing candles. A man wearing a white wig and a frock coat walked by. Max and Dani looked around uncertainly. Suddenly Dani's eyes went wide.

"Jackpot!" she said, stepping over to a big iron cauldron filled with candy. She started to fill her sack. Max was just about to join her when he heard the staircase above them creak. Looking up, he saw a beautiful girl at the top of the staircase. Her light brown hair was pulled into a bun, and she was wearing a gorgeous old-fashioned gown made of rose-colored silk.

"Allison?" Max's jaw dropped.

Dani quickly looked up. "Not *the* Allison?" she whispered.

Max nodded. Allison smiled down at them.

"I thought you weren't into Halloween," she said as she started down the steps.

"I'm, er, taking my sister Dani around," Max replied.

"Well, that's nice of you," Allison said.

"I always do it," Max said.

"My parents made him," Dani added.

Max gave Dani a look, and Allison laughed. She reached the bottom of the steps and turned to a punch bowl filled with cider.

"Want some?" she asked, filling a cup and handing it to Max.

"Uh, sure, thanks," Max said. "So how's the party?"

"Boring." Allison shrugged. "It's just a bunch of my parents' friends. They do this every year, and I get candy duty. By the way, Dani, I love your costume."

"I love yours, too," Dani said. "Of course, I can't wear anything like that because I don't have"—she turned to Max—"don't you call them yabos, Max?"

Allison laughed, and Max practically choked on his cider.

"Your costume looks really authentic," Allison told Dani. "I'm really into witches."

"Me, too," Dani said excitedly. "We just learned about those sisters in school."

"The Sanderson sisters?" Allison asked. "I know all

about them. My mom used to run the museum in the old Sanderson house."

"There's a museum about them?" Dani looked surprised.

"They shut it down," Allison said. "Too many spooky things happened there."

Trying to think of a way to spend some more time with Allison, Max suddenly had an idea. "If it's supposed to be so boogy-boogy scary, why don't we go up there? After all, tonight's the perfect night."

"Well . . ." Allison seemed uncertain.

"Maybe you'll make a believer out of me," Max said hopefully.

"Okay, but I'll have to change clothes," Allison said, and went back upstairs. Dani turned to Max. Her eyes were wide, and her lower lip was quivering.

"There's no way I'm going up there, Max," she said with a trembling voice. "The kids at school told me about that place. It's supposed to be really weird."

Max quickly glanced upstairs, then back at his sister. "This is the girl of my dreams," he whispered.

"So take her to the movies like a normal person," Dani whispered back.

"Please," Max begged. "Do this one thing for me and I'll do anything you say."

Dani thought it over. "Okay, next year we go trick-or-treating as Wendy and Peter Pan."

It took Max a moment to realize what that meant.

"I have to wear . . . tights?" He practically choked on the word.

Dani nodded. "Green ones."

Max took a deep breath. It sounded worse than death. But it wasn't until next year. In the meantime he could get to know Allison better. "Okay, it's a deal."

Allison came back downstairs wearing a beige sweater and jeans. Her hair was now down around her shoulders.

The three of them left Allison's house and were soon climbing the hill toward the Sandersons'. A thin mist hung in the air, and the light of the full moon glowed through the treetops. Allison held Dani's hand. Ahead was a wooden sign covered with peeling paint:

Sanderson House, Circa 1660.
Home of Winifred, Mary, and Sarah Sanderson.
Open Noon 'til 5:00 P.M. Mon–Sat.
Donation 50 Cents.

On the ground next to it lay another, newer sign that had fallen over: Closed! No Trespassing! They stopped and looked up at the dark house.

"My mom used to run this place," Allison said. "But tourists kept having heart attacks and accidents. Finally, the town closed it."

"Well, now we've seen it," Dani said nervously. "So we can go."

The house looked old and creepier than Max had expected. The brick chimney was bent, one of the shutters hung loosely from a window, and some of the roof tiles were missing. Dried leaves made a rustling sound as they swirled in a sudden gust. Max hesitated, but he knew if they turned back now, Allison might decide to go home. Besides, he didn't want to look like a wimp.

"Wait," he said. "Let's take a closer look."

They started toward the house. An old waterwheel stood beside it, but the stream that fed the wheel had dried up long before. As they got closer, Max saw that the windows were made of old wavy glass and gave off weird, distorted reflections.

Suddenly something small and dark shot across their path.

"What was that?" Dani gasped.

Max and Allison looked around. On the path near the front door, a pair of yellow eyes glistened in the moonlight.

"It's just a cat," Max said.

"Not *just* a cat," Allison said. "It's *the* cat. The one that warns you not to go in."

As if it had heard her, the cat yowled. Max picked up a stone and threw it. The cat yelped in pain and disappeared into the shadows.

Allison gave Max a look.

"I didn't mean to hit it," he explained, feeling guilty. "I just wanted to scare it away."

Before Allison could respond, it suddenly grew even darker outside. Max looked up and saw that a cloud was drifting in front of the moon. He really didn't want to go any farther, but he couldn't leave now. Allison probably thought he was a jerk for throwing the rock at that cat. He had to prove to her that he wasn't.

"Let's go inside," Max said.

Dani crossed her arms and shook her head. "No way!"

"Way!" Max said with an exaggerated nod. "I want to take the tour."

"Well, okay," Allison said a little reluctantly. "But we'll only stay a minute." She reached up to the ledge above the front door and found an old key.

The wooden door creaked as it opened. It was so dark inside that Max could hardly see. Dani grabbed Allison's hand and held tight. Max took a step inside. The air smelled stale and musty.

"I can't see anything!" Dani complained.

"There's a light switch here somewhere," Allison said.

Max took another step and felt something small and hard under his foot. He picked it up.

"Hey, I found a lighter!" he said. He tried it, and

the wick caught. The room was lit with its faint, flickering flame.

Across the room, three bent old women suddenly appeared, huddled around a large iron cauldron in the fireplace.

"*Ahhhh!*" Dani screamed in terror, and Max jumped. At that moment Allison found the light switch. The room was flooded with light, and they could see the old women more clearly.

"They're fake," Allison said.

Max turned to his sister. "See? They're just dummies, dummy."

Dani stuck her tongue out at him and looked around. The room was from another era. The floors, walls, and ceiling were made of old wooden planks. Everything had a silvery layer of dust on it, and heavy cobwebs spanned the corners.

Dried animal bones and shriveled clumps of herbs hung from the rafters. The dusty shelves along the walls were filled with oddly shaped blue and brown glass bottles. The only modern addition to the room was a red carpet bordered by gold velvet ropes that led visitors through the house.

Max picked up one of the old bottles and shook it. "Wow, there's still liquid in it."

"Probably some kind of potion," Allison said.

"Uh, yeah, right." Max pretended he believed that.

Dani stepped cautiously toward the three dummies and stared at the one with the red hair.

"That's Winifred, the eldest sister," said Allison. "Her father was a warlock." She pointed to a chubby woman whose dark hair curled like a horn on top of her head. "This is Mary, the middle sister. Her father was a bloodhound. She could follow the scent of a child for miles."

"Is this Sarah?" Dani pointed at the youngest and prettiest of the three. Sarah had a shapely figure and beautiful thick blond hair.

"Yes," said Allison. "The strange one. She would lure children—usually young boys—into the woods to play, and they would never be seen again."

Allison stepped up to a glass case. Inside was an ancient-looking book about the width of a big dictionary. The cover looked moldy, and the edges of its thick pages were brownish and tattered. She read from a small placard on the case:

> The spell book of Winifred Sanderson, given to her by the Devil himself. It contains the recipes for her most powerful and evil spells. The book is said to be bound in the skin of a human child.

"Ahhhh!" Dani screamed again, making them all jump.

"Now what?" Max asked, annoyed.

"Something just ran between my legs!" Dani gasped.

"It's just that stupid cat," Max said. He started to look around again. His eyes stopped on a huge, lone candle, and he read the placard on the stand beneath it:

The Black Flame Candle, made from the fat of a hanged man. Legend says that it will raise the spirits of the dead when lit by a virgin on Halloween night.

The room was suddenly aglow with moonlight coming through the windows. Dani jumped again, and even Allison looked nervous.

"Chill, guys. It's just the moon coming out from behind a cloud," Max said, still looking at the candle. He knew he had a chance to look really brave. "What do you say we light this thing and meet the old broads?"

He raised the lighter toward the candle, but before he could light it, the black cat leapt out of the darkness and clawed his back with a yowl.

"Hey, get this thing off me!" Max shouted, twisting and swinging his arms. The cat fell to the floor and scampered away. Max flicked the lighter.

"Max! No!" Allison and Dani shouted together as the flame leapt out of the lighter and Max held it to the candle.

"Oh, come on," Max said. "I'm going to prove to you once and for all that this is all just a bunch of hocus pocus."

THE CAT LET OUT another shrieking yowl, but it was too late. The flame from the lighter touched the candle's wick.

Ker-pow! Every light bulb in the room exploded. A dark wind raced around the room, kicking up dust and tearing the cobwebs from the corners. Max, Dani, and Allison instinctively ducked.

"Ahhh-hah-hah-hah-hah-hah-haaaaaa . . ." Cruel cackling laughter filled the room.

As suddenly as they'd started, the wind and laughter stopped. The room became still. Max's heart was beating like a drum.

"What happened?" he whispered.

"A virgin just lit the candle," Dani whispered back.

Max heard Allison chuckle. Sometimes he wished Dani wasn't so smart for her age. Anyway, maybe the lights blowing out was just a coincidence. For Allison's sake, he tried to act brave.

"Uh, right," he said, looking up. "And look, nothing hap—"

Before he could finish the sentence, the door flew open, and a woman with red hair stepped into the room. Max's eyes almost popped out of his head when he saw that her black-and-red gown was smoldering as if she'd just stepped from the flames of hell. Dani crawled under a table, and Allison quickly scurried into a shadowy corner. Max hid in a broom closet, squeezing in beside a vacuum cleaner, a dust mop, and some old straw brooms.

The woman stepped into the room and looked around as if she was glad to be home. Behind her came a chubbier woman with black hair, and then a younger, shapely woman with thick blond hair. Max couldn't believe his eyes. They looked exactly like the three Sanderson dummies!

"Ah, sweet revenge!" the red-haired woman exclaimed. "My curse worked perfectly."

"Because thou art perfect, Winnie," said the chubby one.

Winnie is short for Winifred, Max thought with a

tremble. Like Winifred Sanderson. . . . No, it couldn't be!

"But who lit the candle?" Winifred asked.

Sarah Sanderson pulled up a loose floorboard and lifted something from beneath it. "My lucky rat tail!" she screeched. "Just where I left it!"

Max felt his jaw drop. It *was* them! He watched in amazement as Mary stepped toward the dummies of herself and her sisters.

"Oh, look," she giggled. "Are these not clever, Sisters? They appear so lifelike."

"That doth not look anything like me," Winifred said, turning up her nose.

"Well, of course not, Sister," Mary said with what seemed to Max to be fake sweetness. "They have missed that special glow of thy skin and the way—"

Whack! Winifred smacked Mary across the back of her head.

"They made her much too old," Winifred informed her sister.

It seemed to Max that the Winifred dummy looked about the same age as the real one. Winifred turned and stepped toward the glass case where the spell book lay.

"Wake up, my sleepy one," she said, tapping the glass gently. "Did thou miss me? I missed thee."

With a crash she thrust her hands through the glass

and lifted the book out. Max couldn't believe what he was seeing. It was definitely time to leave. But how?

"Come, my darling," Winifred cooed to her book. "We have work to do!"

"Wait!" Mary gasped, sniffing loudly. "I smell children. One is most definitely a young girl. Seven . . . maybe eight years old."

The three witches quickly began to scan the room. Max backed farther into the closet.

"Let's play with her," Sarah said with a wicked smile.

"Come out, my dear," Winifred called in a singsong voice. "We shall not harm thee."

"Yes," Mary added, licking her lips. "We love children."

Winifred suddenly upended the table Dani was hiding under. Max's sister cowered for a moment, then looked down at her Halloween costume and compared it with those of the witches.

"I thought thou would never come, Sisters," she said, rising bravely and pretending to be a witch, also. Max couldn't believe how gutsy she was.

"Greetings, little one," Winifred said with a knowing smile.

" 'Twas I who brought you back," Dani said.

The three witches gathered around her, pawing at her hair and poking her with their fingers.

"Such a pretty little"—Winifred seemed to choke on the next word—"child."

"And so well fed," Mary said, squeezing one of Dani's arms.

"Tell me, dumpling," Winifred said, leaning closer. "What is the year?"

"N-n-nineteen ninety-three," Dani stammered fearfully.

Winifred straightened up. "Sisters, we have been dead . . . three hundred years!"

"My, how time flies," Mary giggled.

"Especially when you're dead!" Sarah cried.

The witches howled with laughter. Dani joined in. Max felt a sickening sensation in his stomach. He doubted the witches believed Dani's act.

"Well, I guess I'll be going," Dani said, taking a step toward the door. Winifred quickly blocked her path.

"Oh, do stay for dinner, dearest," she said.

"I . . . I'm not hungry," Dani gasped.

"But we are!" Mary grabbed her. Max knew he had to do something.

"Hey!" he shouted, jumping out from the closet. "Let go of my sister!"

The next thing Max knew, Winifred whirled around and pointed her bony hands at him.

ZAAAAAPPPPP! Max felt a sudden shock as if he'd

touched a live electrical wire. He was lifted off the ground, unable to break free of the electrical force.

"Roast him, Winnie!" Mary urged.

"No, let *me* play with him," Sarah said, moving closer.

"You leave my brother alone!" Dani swung her candy sack at Winifred, knocking her sideways. A second later Max crumpled to the floor in a daze.

Winifred turned to grab Dani, but the black cat leapt onto the witch's shoulder and clawed her. Mary reached for the cat, but Allison jumped out of the shadows and punched Mary in the nose.

"Here, kitty, kitty!" Sarah giggled in the middle of the fracas.

Still on the floor, Max slowly came to his senses. It was becoming obvious that they didn't stand a chance against the witches. They had to get out of there fast! He looked up and noticed another modern addition to the old house.

"Beware!" he shouted, jumping up on a table and flicking his lighter again. The three witches suddenly stopped and stared at him.

"You have messed with the great and powerful Max!" he shouted, holding the lighter's flame up to the indoor sprinkler system. "You must now suffer the consequences! I summon the Burning Rain of Death!"

Briinnnggg! Somewhere in the house a fire alarm

40

went off. *Fwooosh!* The sprinkler started spraying water all over the room.

"The Burning Rain of Death!" Sarah shrieked in terror.

As Max jumped off the table, he came face-to-face with the black cat.

"Nice move, Max," the cat said.

"Huh?" Max stared at it in disbelief. First real witches, now a talking cat?

"Right, I talk," the cat said. "Now get the spell book and let's scram!"

The witches were racing around, trying to escape the Burning Rain of Death. Dani and Allison headed for the door. Max grabbed the book and followed. As he ran from the house, he could hear Winifred scream, "It's only water! The boy hath tricked us and stolen my book! After them, Sisters!"

Max dashed down the hill. Ahead, near the street, he could see the cat motioning Allison and Dani to hide in the shadow between two parked cars. The girls ducked down, and Max joined them.

"Are you Thackery Binx?" Allison whispered to the cat.

"No, I'm Garfield's long-lost cousin," the cat hissed. "Now be quiet!"

Crouching between the cars, Max still couldn't believe what was going on. Witches and a talking cat? He pinched himself. It hurt. This wasn't a dream.

A few moments later the three witches reached the edge of the street and stopped.

"A black river!" Mary gasped.

"What is that?" Sarah asked, pointing at the car Max and the others were hiding behind. Winifred stepped toward the car. Max held his breath as the witch bent down and squinted.

" 'Tis a Ford," Winifred said. "Obviously a vessel for fording this river."

"What shall we do?" Mary asked.

"Perhaps it is not deep," Sarah said, sticking her toe out tentatively. Winifred and Mary shared a look and pushed Sarah off the curb.

"Help!" Sarah shrieked as she stumbled into the street. "I cannot swim!" Then she realized she wasn't sinking.

" 'Tis firm as stone," Winifred said, stepping into the street. "I believe it is a road."

The witches quickly hurried across the street. As soon as they were gone, the cat jumped away from the car and headed in the opposite direction.

"Come on," he hissed.

"Wait a minute, Binx," Max said. "Where are you taking us?"

Binx stared back at them with yellow eyes. "The graveyard."

A LIGHT MIST FLOATED over the graveyard, and the moonlight cast weird shadows among the trees. Thin and flat, many of the gravestones leaned to one side. To Max the whole scene was not only totally bizarre but creepy, too.

"Why did we have to come here?" Max asked.

"This is the one place where the Sanderson sisters can't touch us," Binx replied.

"Get serious," Max muttered.

"I am," Binx replied.

"You're saying I have to spend the rest of my life in a graveyard?"

"Not the rest of your life," Binx said. "Just until dawn."

"Why dawn?" Allison asked as they walked past the graves.

"If the Sanderson sisters don't steal the life of a child by the first light, they'll evaporate," Binx explained. "If we can keep the spell book away from them until dawn, the witches basically get nuked."

"Hey," Max said, "if you're from the old days like those witches, how come you don't talk like them?"

"Because unlike them, I've been *alive* for the past three hundred years."

Allison suddenly stopped and brought her hand to her mouth. "Oh my God!" she gasped.

"What's wrong?" Max asked.

"It's Halloween. There are children everywhere tonight."

"Oh man, the Sanderson sisters will have a feast," Max groaned.

"This is all your fault, Max," Dani said.

"*My* fault?" Max said. "Who's the one who made me go trick-or-treating?"

"*Who* lit the candle?" Allison asked, half accusingly and half teasing.

"*Who* took us up to the house?" Max shot back.

"Hey!" Binx snapped. "Can we fight about this later?"

"Ahh!" Dani gasped, then froze. Max bumped into

her and looked up to find a skeleton holding a long knifelike scythe. It took a second for them to realize it was only an engraving on a tall old gravestone. The inscription read: William Butcherson. Lost Soul.

"Billy Butcherson was Winifred's lover," Binx explained, jumping on top of an old tombstone. "But she found him sporting with her sister Sarah."

"Sporting?" Dani repeated, puzzled.

Allison and Max glanced at each other. "It's like when you have one girlfriend, but you mess around with someone else," Max tried to explain.

"Oh! You mean Billy *cheated* on Winifred," Dani said. "Why didn't you just say so?"

Binx cleared his throat. "Anyway, when Winifred found out, she poisoned Billy and then sewed his lips shut with a dull needle so he couldn't tell her secrets, even in death."

"I guess Winifred is the jealous type," Allison said.

"Uh, yes," Binx said. "Now please sit down. There's a lot you should know before the fun begins."

"Fun?" Max scowled.

"Okay, it was a poor choice of words," Binx admitted. "Now please sit."

Dani and Allison sat, but Max remained standing. It was still hard for him to believe that a cat who had once been Thackery Binx was talking to them. Not only that, but he was giving them orders! Max realized that Binx was staring at him.

"You have a problem?" Binx asked.

"Uh, no." Max sat.

"This is your sister's headstone, isn't it?" Allison asked, pointing at the headstone Binx was perched on. The faint inscription read: Emily Binx.

"Yes," the cat said. "Because of me, my little sister's life was stolen. For years I waited for my life as a cat to end so that I could be reunited with her in death. But Winifred's curse of immortality kept me alive. I watched my parents and all my friends grow old and die. I was miserable. Then one day I realized my immortality gave me a purpose. I'd failed Emily, but I wouldn't fail again. So for three centuries I've guarded the Sanderson house on Halloween to stop any airhead virgins from lighting the Black Flame Candle and bringing the sisters back."

Max realized they were all staring at him.

"Nice going, airhead," Dani muttered.

"Hey, I'm sorry, okay?" Max said defensively. "But we're talking about three old hags versus the twentieth century. How bad can it be?"

"Bad," Binx said. "Believe me."

Max, Allison, and Dani gave each other nervous looks.

"Maybe this could help." Allison took the spell book from Max and started to open it.

"Hey!" Binx yelled. "Stay out of there!"

Allison quickly shut the book.

"Never open that book again," Binx warned. "It contains all of Winifred's most powerful spells. Whatever we do, we can't let her get her claws on it."

"So why are we messing around?" Max asked, taking the book back from Allison and pulling out his lighter. "Let's just torch the sucker. Then those witches will never be able to steal any lives. Stand back, everyone. This baby's gonna burn."

The flame burst out of the lighter, but before Max could touch it to the book, the book exhaled. A big ball of fire exploded in front of Max's face.

"Yikes!" Max jumped back, dropping the book. His eyebrows were singed.

"It's protected by magic," Binx explained.

"Why didn't you warn me?" Max asked.

"Why did you throw that rock at me before?" Binx replied, licking his paw.

Suddenly they heard evil laughter and looked up. The three witches were hovering directly above them on old straw brooms. Max and the others cowered on the ground.

"Why didn't you warn me? Why didn't you warn me?" Sarah and Mary mimicked Max.

"Still think it's all just a bunch of hocus pocus?" Winifred asked with an evil grin. Max realized Allison was watching him.

"Yo, hags!" he shouted, trying to look brave. "Get lost!"

Winifred stared down at him. Max felt as if she were staring straight into his soul. It sent a shiver through him.

"Ah, it's the brave little virgin who lit the candle," Winifred said with a leer. "He misses his friends. He wants to go home."

"Boo-hoo-hoo!" Mary and Sarah pretended to cry. Max felt totally humiliated. Then Sarah dipped toward him.

"I'll be thy friend," she said with an enticing wink.

"Take a hike!" Allison shouted at her. Max turned and smiled at Allison, who looked away.

"She's jealous," Winifred said. "And isn't she pretty? Almost as pretty as her ancestor, little Elizabeth Podbury, the good witch."

"Good to the very last bite!" Mary cried, licking her lips.

The witches cackled with wicked glee. Then Winifred reached out with her hand. "Book!" she cried.

The spell book started to rise off the ground, but Binx jumped off the tombstone and landed on it, pinning it to the earth.

Winifred's eyes narrowed. "Thackery Binx! Still alive?"

"And waiting for you," Binx replied.

"You've waited in vain," Winifred snapped. "You will fail to save thy friends . . . just as you failed to save thy sister!"

Max had never seen a cat flinch before, but he was certain Binx did then. Above them the witches began to chant. "Ickie-tao . . . ickie-too-tao . . . ickie-tee-tao . . ."

"Don't listen to them!" Allison shouted, covering her ears. Dani and Max quickly did the same.

"Blast them!" Winifred shouted. She and her sisters swooped downward on their broomsticks, but the kids ducked and flattened themselves on the cold ground. The witches flew back up into the sky and huddled for a moment. Max gave Binx a nervous look.

"As long as we stay here, they can't touch us, right?" he asked nervously.

"*They* can't," Binx replied.

"I don't like the way you said that," Dani said nervously.

Above them Winifred called out:

> Unfaithful lover, long since dead.
> Deep asleep in a wormy bed.
> Wiggle toe, open eye.
> Twist thy fingers toward the sky.
> Life is sweet, so don't be shy.
> On thy feet! says I—says I!

As Max watched, Winifred pulled the Black Flame Candle out of her cape and blew on it. A flame burst onto the wick. Suddenly the ground beneath Max began to rumble. He and the others jumped to their feet. The tombstone over Billy Butcherson's grave fell backward, and the ground bulged. Jagged shards of wood from an old coffin shot up through the earth.

Then a body sat up.

"Billy Butcherson!" Allison gasped. Dani jumped behind Max and hugged him in terror. Billy looked very gaunt and bony. His skin was gray, his hair long and frizzy. He was wearing an ancient moldy frock coat, and his lips *were* sewn together!

"He's a zombie!" Dani cried.

The stench of rotten flesh wafted into Max's nose.

"And he stinks, too!" Max said.

The kids watched in terror as Billy looked around with sleepy eyes, then lay back down in his coffin.

"Get up, you rotter!" Winifred screamed and gave him a jolt of electricity. With an angry groan, Billy sat up again.

"Oh, Billy," Sarah sighed forlornly for her old boyfriend.

Whack! Winifred smacked her and then shouted at Billy. "Catch those children!"

Billy turned and stared at the kids. He pulled himself to his feet and began to stagger toward them.

"Is this for real?" Max stammered, backing away.

"You better believe it!" Binx shouted, starting to run. "Follow me! And don't forget the spell book."

"But we can't leave the graveyard!" Max yelled as he grabbed the book.

"Just do what he says, Max!" Dani said.

They started to run through the tombstones and trees. The witches hovered over them, and Billy followed, picking up speed. Max looked back and realized the zombie was gaining on them. He stopped and grabbed a tree branch, bending it way back. As Billy staggered toward him with his bony hands outstretched, Max let go of the branch.

Crack! The branch swung back and hit Billy in the face, knocking his head clear off his body. Billy's head rolled behind a tree, and his body flopped to the ground. Max stopped and let out a big sigh of relief. One less zombie to worry about.

Then Billy's body rose to its hands and knees and started groping around for its head. Max stared in disbelief, then turned and ran.

Ahead, Binx was nearing the graveyard wall. The witches hovered above it on their broomsticks, waiting with evil grins on their faces. Dani and Allison were following close behind Binx, but Max slowed down.

"Come on!" Binx shouted.

"But the witches—," Max gasped.

"Just do it, Max!" Allison yelled.

Binx approached the wall. Sarah hovered just beyond it.

"Here, kitty, kitty!" she called.

Just before Binx reached the wall, he disappeared

behind a clump of brambles. A second later Dani and Allison disappeared, too. But Max hesitated.

"Blast that Thackery Binx!" Winifred shrieked. "Blast him! Blast him!"

"Blast him! Blast him! Blast him!" Mary and Sarah chanted.

Whack! Whack! Winifred smacked her sisters. On the ground below, it looked to Max as if the witches had a real Three Stooges routine going.

Suddenly Max smelled something disgusting. He spun around. Billy was right behind him! He'd put his head back on, but it was twisted too far to the left, so he could only stare at Max out of the corners of his eyes.

Still clutching the spell book, Max took a step back. His heart was pounding, and he couldn't breathe. He felt paralyzed with fear as the zombie's long, dirty fingernails reached toward him.

5

AT THE LAST SECOND, Max turned and dived behind the brambles. He fell through a hole in the ground and slid down the loose dirt into the dark.

A moment later he hit bottom. He was in some sort of cavern. It was pitch black and smelled like fresh, moist dirt. Max could hear people breathing. He pulled out his lighter and lit it. Allison, Dani, and Binx stared back at him in the flickering light.

Max looked up and felt his blood turn cold. They were under the graveyard. Corners of coffins poked out of the cavern ceiling, along with bony hands and feet.

"Charming," Allison groaned with a shiver.

53

"Don't worry, I've hunted moles down here for years," Binx said.

"Moles? Yuck!" Dani made a face.

"Hey," Binx said. "You don't know till you've tried 'em."

"Are you okay?" Max asked Allison.

She nodded. "I guess, all things considered."

Dani sniffed. "What's that disgusting smell?"

A second later they heard groaning and footsteps coming toward them.

"It's Mildew Man!" Allison cried, jumping up.

"This way!" Binx shouted, and they all ran.

The cavern led into a sewer tunnel. Fortunately, it was dry. Max held up his lighter as he and Binx led the way.

"We must be out of the graveyard now," Max said as they ran. "Does this thing ever end?"

"Hold the lighter higher," Dani said behind him. "I can't see."

By accident the lighter scraped against the wall. The flame went out, and once again they were plunged into darkness.

"Ahhhhh!" Dani screamed, sending shivers up Max's spine.

"Dani!" he shouted angrily as he relit the lighter. "Will you stop doing that?"

"She's only seven," Allison said, defending Max's little sister. "This is scary. Give her a break!"

"Yeah." Dani sniffed. "Give me a break."

"Excuse me," Binx said. "Do you think you could work this out later?"

Max shrugged. It seemed like he kept messing up, especially as far as Allison was concerned. Farther down the tunnel, they came to some metal rungs leading up to a manhole cover. Max handed the spell book to Allison and started to climb up. Binx jumped on his shoulder. Max reached the top and pushed up the manhole cover. He looked around and realized they had come up in the middle of a street. A pair of headlights was bearing down on him! He quickly dropped back down into the tunnel just as a car rolled over the manhole.

Max hit the floor hard and stumbled into Allison's arms. For a moment he held her close as they looked into each other's eyes.

"Ahem." Dani cleared her throat. Max stepped away and looked back up at the manhole cover.

"That was close," he said.

"Where's Binx?" Allison asked.

"He must have jumped off my shoulder just before I ducked," Max said, climbing up again. He pushed open the manhole cover. There were no cars coming, so he climbed out. The girls followed. They stood on the street, looking around for the cat.

"I know he wouldn't just leave us," Allison said.

"Oh no!" Dani cried, pointing down. Binx lay quietly a few feet away, his body flattened to the road.

"He must have been run over by the car," Max said.

"Poor kitty!" Dani sniffed.

Max felt terrible. "I'm sorry, Dani. It's all my fault."

"Wait!" Allison gasped. "Look!"

They watched in total amazement as Binx's head and feet began to twitch. The cat started to inflate like a balloon: First his toes; then his legs and tail; finally, his body and head. Binx turned his head back and forth as if getting the kinks out. A moment later he was like new.

"Don't you hate when that happens?" Binx asked.

"I wouldn't know," Max replied.

Down the street a bus stopped at a traffic light.

"If we get on it, we can get away from Billy the Zombie," Allison said.

"Good idea," Max said.

They ran down to the bus stop and waited anxiously for the light to change. A moment later the bus started toward them. Max saw something strange inside. It looked as if a woman with blond hair was sitting on the bus driver's lap, steering.

"Oh no!" Max gasped. He quickly grabbed Dani and dived behind a hedge. Allison and Binx followed. The bus stopped, and the doors opened. Max stared through the hedge and saw Sarah give the bus driver a kiss on the cheek and slide off his lap.

56

Salem, Massachusetts, Halloween night, 1693—the interior of the Sanderson house, the home of three sisters suspected of being witches.

Winifred, one of the Sanderson sisters, stirs the bubbling brew she will give to Emily Binx.

Thackery Binx receives a jolt from Winifred when he tries to save Emily.

After robbing Emily of her life and turning Thackery into an immortal black cat, the three witches are hanged by the townsfolk.

Salem, Massachusetts, Halloween night, 1993—Max Dennison and his sister, Dani, run into Ernie, the town bully.

Things seem to be looking up for Max when he and Dani accidentally find Allison's house.

Max, Allison, and Dani decide to visit the witch museum in the creepy old Sanderson house.

Max accidentally brings the sisters back to life, and they are delighted to be reunited with Winifred's old spell book.

After being discovered by the Sanderson sisters, Dani pretends to be a fellow witch.

Binx, now over three hundred years old, is not only immortal, but he can talk, too! He decides to help the kids stop the witches.

Max and Dani show up at the town's adult Halloween party and unsuccessfully try to get help from their parents.

Allison and Max discover that a ring of salt can protect them from the witches.

When the witches are finally defeated, Thackery's spirit is released, and Dani gets to keep a great black cat!

"Hey, don't I get your phone number?" the bus driver asked. "You want my route schedule?"

"Thou wouldst hate me in the morning," Sarah said teasingly.

"No, I wouldn't," the bus driver said.

"Believe me, thou wouldst," Winifred said, pulling Sarah off the bus.

The driver shook his head and sighed. "Story of my life. They get on, they get off."

He closed the door and pulled away, leaving the witches at the bus stop. A bunch of kids in costumes were heading toward them.

Mary took a deep sniff. "I smell children."

"What are *they*?" Sarah asked, pointing at the turtles, army men, and bats walking past with bags of candy.

"Hobgoblins," Winifred guessed. Mary was still sniffing frantically.

"I am all confused, Sisters," Mary lamented. "I *smell* children, but I don't *see* any. Is it possible I've lost my powers?"

"What will we do without our powers?" Sarah whimpered.

She and Mary hugged each other in fear. Winifred gave them an annoyed look.

"Enough of this whimpering!" she shouted. "We are witches! We are evil. What would Mother say if she saw us like this?"

"Mother . . ." Mary and Sarah sighed sadly and hung their heads.

Whack! Whack! Winifred snapped them out of it with two quick smacks to the head.

"What are we?" she demanded.

"Witches," Sarah and Mary replied.

"And what do we want?" Winifred asked like a cheerleader.

"Children!" Mary and Sarah seemed less afraid.

"When do we want them?" Winifred asked.

"Now!" Sarah and Mary were gung ho.

"Snake formation!" Winifred shouted.

The next thing Max knew, the witches lined up and headed toward the hedge, single file. Max and the others shrunk back into the shadows. The sisters passed, muttering a childhood chant:

> Satan loves us, this we know.
> Because our mother told us so.
> And when in trouble, be smart ladies.
> Do not waste time, go straight to
>   Hades.

They crossed the lawn of the house behind the bus stop and left their brooms leaning on a tree outside. Max turned and watched. Something about the house looked familiar.

"We were there," Dani whispered. "That's the Devil's house."

They watched the front door swing open and heard the horror music start to play as the man in the devil costume came out.

"Master!" The three witches fell to their knees before him.

"You must be the Sanderson sisters," the Devil said.

"We are," said Winifred.

"I was expecting you," the Devil said. "Come on in and take a load off."

The witches went into the house. Max and the others turned to Binx.

"What should we do?" Allison asked.

"Take their brooms," Binx said. "At least that will make it harder for them to find us."

Max and Allison glanced at each other and nodded. They sneaked up to the tree, grabbed the brooms, and ran back to the street.

"What should we do with them?" Max whispered.

"Look," Allison said. Three young girls dressed as the Sanderson sisters were coming toward them, carrying cardboard brooms.

"Hey," Allison said, holding up the real brooms, "want to trade?"

The girls' eyes went wide. "Oh, cool. Neat brooms!" They eagerly made the exchange and ran off. Allison and Max left the cardboard brooms near the tree and rejoined Binx and Dani.

"Let's get out of here," Binx whispered.

Still clutching the spell book tightly, Max followed the others down the dark sidewalk, past groups of trick-or-treaters.

"Don't forget," Binx said. "They can't do anything without the spell book. We have to keep it out of their hands."

"But they're still witches," Max said. "How long can we do that?"

"Maybe *he* can help us," Dani said. She pointed at a brightly lit convenience store up the street. A motorcycle cop was leaning on a motorcycle parked outside. They ran toward him.

"Officer! Officer!" Dani shouted.

The cop didn't look happy to see her. "What's the problem?"

"Okay, it's like this," Max began, still gasping for breath from running. "We broke into the old Sanderson house and accidentally brought the witches back from the dead."

"You lit the Black Flame Candle?" The cop raised an eyebrow.

"Yes."

"You're really a virgin?" the cop asked.

Max couldn't believe what a big deal everyone was making about it. Out of the corner of his eye, he saw Allison start to smile. "Yeah, I'm a virgin," he told the cop. "I'll have it tattooed on my back, okay?"

"The point is, the witches are after us," Dani said.

60

"We need police protection," said Allison.

Making circles in the air with his hands, the cop started to chant, "Hamma dooma damma dooma dinga damma dooma. . . ."

Max and the others scowled at each other.

"That's police magic," the cop explained. "You are now protected from witches for the next twenty-four hours."

Allison put her hands on her hips. "Officer, this is *not* a prank."

"Hey!" The cop suddenly looked angry. "Every day I put my life on the line for the people of this community, and you punks pull this! Now get out of here, and take that cat with you!"

Dani picked up Binx and started to run. Max and Allison followed her to an empty yard, where she sat down under a tree and began to sob. They crouched beside her.

"I can't believe that a cop wouldn't help us," Max said, stroking his sister's head.

"I guess on Halloween night we must have sounded like the boy who cried wolfman," Allison said.

Suddenly they heard a roar, and the motorcycle cop shot past them on the street. A woman wearing a tight leopard-print dress was riding behind him.

"Something tells me he wasn't a cop after all," Allison said. "That must have just been some guy in costume."

"I wanna go home!" Dani sobbed. "I want Mom and Dad!"

Allison gave Max a worried look. Max nodded and turned to his sister.

"Look, Dani—," Max started to stay.

"Leave me alone!" Dani shouted.

Max sighed. He knew he wouldn't be able to change her mind. "Okay, you're right," he said. "I think it's time to go crash another party."

"The one Mom and Dad are at?" Dani asked through her tears.

Max nodded, and Dani started to smile a little.

"Hey, I knew you could smile," Max said. "But I need you to be very brave tonight. We have to be real tough. Like the night Grandma got sick. Remember?"

Dani nodded and wiped a tear from her cheek with her hand.

"I need you to be that tough tonight," Max said. "Don't forget. It's gonna be real hard to get anyone to believe us."

"Okay," Dani said with a sniff. "I just wish I had my doll."

Binx rubbed against her and purred. "Tonight, you have me."

Dani smiled and picked him up. Allison caught Max's eye and nodded in appreciation. It seemed that being brave didn't impress her as much as being thoughtful. Dani started to pet Binx.

"Oh, yeah," Binx groaned in delight. "That feels great. Now do my other ear. Oh, yes, my tummy . . . that's great!"

Max felt a tug on his sleeve. Allison was pointing at two girls coming toward them. They were both dressed as ballerinas and were sucking on stick candies.

"They're my neighbors," Allison said. "I think we better start telling kids to stay off the streets."

"You really think they'll listen to us?" Max asked.

"Well, we can try," Allison said, turning toward the girls. "Hey, Cindy. Hey, Donna."

The girls didn't respond. They seemed to be in a daze. Allison stepped right in front of one of them. "Cindy?"

"Oh, uh, hi, Allison," Cindy mumbled, and held the candy out. "You should try this. It's really great candy."

Allison took the candy, and the girls started to walk away.

"It's shaped like a crow," Max said, joining her.

Hearing that, Binx ran over. "It's the same candy they gave my sister before they stole her life!"

Allison spun around and yelled, "Hey, Cindy, where'd you get this?"

"In the park up the hill," Cindy replied without turning around.

"I bet the witches made this!" Binx said.

Max caught Allison's eye. "I have a feeling it's too late to tell kids to stay off the streets."

"We better see what's going on," Binx said.

They ran up the hill and hid behind some trees. The Sanderson sisters were thirty feet away in a small park, surrounded by children.

"Trick or treat!" Sarah said cheerfully as she gave out the crow-shaped candies. "Trick or treat!"

The children pressed eagerly around the witches. "Gimme some!" they cried. "Gimme! Gimme!"

"Stop pawing me, you little brats!" Winifred snapped.

"Remember to share with thy neighbors," Mary said.

"You're ugly," a kid said to Winifred. The witch angrily shoved a piece of candy into his mouth.

"Eat this," she said.

Behind the trees Max and the others watched as the kids gobbled up the candy.

"Once they taste that candy, they're under the witches' spell," Binx whispered.

"They're going to steal *all* their lives," Dani gasped. Allison gave Max a worried look.

"Not if they can't get this book," Max said bravely, squeezing the book in his arms.

A strong odor wafted over them.

"Do you smell something?" Allison whispered.

"It can't be Billy," Max whispered back. "We left him in the sewer."

Binx turned around. "Uh, I think he got out."

The kids turned and screamed. Rotten Billy Butcherson was standing right behind them! Max and the others took off down the hill. Winifred turned and saw them.

"After them!" she shrieked to her sisters. "Get my book!"

THE SALEM TOWN HALL was located in a big brick building in the middle of town. As Max and the others approached it, they could hear loud music coming from inside. The windows were brightly lit, and people dressed as pirates, princesses, and presidential candidates were hanging around on the front steps.

Inside, the place was packed. Cardboard skeletons and ghosts made from pillows and sheets lined the walls. Tables were piled high with pumpkin pies, bowls of candy, and jugs of cider. Up on the stage a band was playing and a singer dressed like Elvis Presley was crooning into a microphone.

Max and the others stared at the crowd.

"And I thought cats were weird," Binx mumbled.

"Mom and Dad must be here somewhere," Max said.

"We'll never find them in this crowd," Dani said.

"Yes we will," Max said. "You and Binx go that way. Allison and I will go this way."

They split up and headed into the crowd. Max took Allison's hand and squeezed it. It felt good when she squeezed back. As they made their way through the dancers, Max suddenly felt a pair of hands go around his neck.

"Ahhh!" he shouted, jumping around.

"Hey, easy," said a white-faced vampire wearing a black cape. "It's just a party."

"Is that you, Dad?" Max asked.

"I am not Dad, I am Dad-cula," Mr. Dennison said with a bad Transylvanian accent. He turned to Allison. "And who is this lovely young blood donor?"

Before Max could reply, his father took Allison's hand and kissed it. "Ummm. Type O. My favorite!"

Now Dani and Binx joined them. A heavily made-up woman wearing an incredibly tight dress and a frightful blond wig also stepped up. A large crucifix hung between two pointed funnel-shaped objects on her chest.

"Mom!" Dani gasped. "What are you supposed to be?"

"Madonna," Mrs. Dennison replied, petting Binx. "What a cute cat."

"Mom, Dad, listen," Max said quickly. "Something really terrible has happened." He told them the story of breaking into the Sanderson house, lighting the Black Flame Candle, and bringing the witches back to life. When he finished, his parents stared at him as if he were crazy.

"It's true, Mom, I swear!" Dani insisted.

"How much candy have you had?" Mrs. Dennison asked, putting her hand on Dani's forehead.

"I haven't OD'd on sugar, Mom," Dani said. "They're real witches."

"You haven't been listening to Ozzy Osbourne again, have you?" Mr. Dennison asked Max.

"This really happened, Dad, I swear it," Max said.

"*We* swear it," Allison added, pointing at Binx. "If you don't believe us, you can ask Binx."

Mr. and Mrs. Dennison looked at the black cat and frowned. Suddenly Dani saw Winifred pushing her way through the crowd.

"Look!" she whispered to Max.

"Hide!" Max whispered back.

Max, Allison, and Dani hid behind Mr. and Mrs. Dennison. A moment later Winifred bumped into Max's mom.

"I beg your pardon!" Mrs. Dennison stiffened.

"Cow!" Winifred snapped.

68

"Witch!" Max's mom snapped back.

"Mom, that's *her*!" Dani whispered.

Not far away, a woman dressed in a white gown and carrying a wand stopped in front of Mary.

"Excuse me," the woman said. "Are you a good witch or a bad witch?"

Urrrrrrppp! Mary reared back and released a belch that was so loud a dozen people turned. The woman in the white gown fainted to the floor. Hearing the commotion, Winifred turned and caught Max's eye.

"She sees us!" Max cried. "Come on!"

Max dashed toward the stage, with Allison and Dani right behind him. Onstage, Max grabbed the microphone away from the singer.

"Hey, everybody!" His voice boomed through the room. "This is an emergency!"

The musicians stopped playing, and the crowd stared at them with confused looks. Still holding Binx, Dani stretched up on her toes to the microphone. "This is not a test!"

"Your kids are in danger!" Max told the audience. "The Sanderson sisters have returned from the grave! *And there they are!*"

Max pointed at the three witches. The crowd stared at them, uncertainly. The Sanderson sisters bared their teeth and pointed their sharp fingernails. The crowd gasped and backed away. All of a sudden Winifred put on a fake smile and began to sing.

Sarah and Mary quickly joined in.

The crowd around them started to smile and applaud. They began to sway to the music, not realizing that it was putting them under a spell.

"It was a joke!" Mrs. Dennison laughed.

Grinning, Mr. Dennison turned toward Max on the stage. "Why, you clever little son of a gun!" he shouted.

But as the witches sang, the adults around the room began to look dazed.

"The spell's working!" Allison gasped.

"Don't listen to them!" Dani screamed.

Suddenly that horrible smell spread over the stage. The kids turned and saw Billy Butcherson lurching toward them. They jumped off the stage and tried to escape through the crowd. Meanwhile, Winifred finished casting her spell on the dancers:

Revenge is sweet, and so am I.
Dance . . . dance until you die!

The band began to play wild, frenzied music, and the entire crowd jumped to their feet and started to dance as if their lives depended on it.

Max and the others made it to the front doors and ran back out into the street. They headed down the block and turned into a dark alley. Exhausted and gasping for breath, they sat against the alley wall. Dani chewed on her thumb, and Allison bit her lip. Max could sense how scared they all were.

"This is really bad," he said.

"No one believes us," Allison said.

"Not even Mom and Dad!" cried Dani. Allison put her arms around Max's little sister and comforted her.

"They would have believed *you*," Max said to Binx.

"I tried to tell them, but . . ." Binx looked down at the ground.

"Cat got your tongue?" Allison asked.

"Very funny," Binx muttered.

Allison looked over at Max. "What are we going to do?"

It made Max feel good that she had asked. "Maybe you should take Dani back to your house. Binx and I will try to handle this."

"No way!" Dani said adamantly. "We're all in this together."

"She's right. It's up to all of us," Allison agreed. "Just because we're not witches doesn't mean we don't have powers of our own." She and Dani gave each other high fives.

"Okay, okay." Max wasn't going to argue. "So what are we gonna do? I mean, how do you destroy evil witches?"

They all looked at one another. No one had an answer.

"Uh oh," Binx said, pointing a paw up the street.

The kids quickly crept to the corner and peered around the wall. Not far away, the witches were approaching. Mary led them, crawling on her hands and knees, sniffing like a dog.

"My nostrils are killing me," she complained.

Thunk! Winifred kicked her in the butt. "Do they feel better now?"

"She's following our scent," Dani whispered.

"We better think of something fast," Max said.

Allison looked around, then pointed at an old stove someone had thrown out in the alley. "There!"

"What?" Max asked.

"That stove," Allison said.

"So?"

"I've got an idea," Allison said. "Follow me!" She started to run. Max and the others followed.

Allison led them down several blocks and across the high school athletic field. Ahead of them loomed the old brick high school, aglow in the moonlight and looking like a big haunted house.

"Why are we going to school?" Max asked as he ran behind her.

"You'll see," Allison said. She reached the outside door that led into the boys locker room.

"Oh, please be open," she prayed, grabbing the door handle. "Darn, it's locked."

"What's the point?" Max asked.

Instead of answering him, Allison stepped to a window near the door. "Get us in, Max. Fast."

"You mean, break in?" Max asked, amazed. "I can't. I'll get in trouble."

"If you don't break in, there won't be anyone left for you to get in trouble with," Allison said.

"Uh, that's a good point." Max looked around and found a rock.

Crash! He threw it through the window, then reached in and undid the latch. A moment later they climbed through the window and into the locker room.

"Ahhhh!" Dani suddenly screamed in terror.

"What is it?" Max gasped.

"That zombie's in here!" Dani cried. "Can't you smell him?"

Max and Allison took deep sniffs.

"That's not the zombie," Allison said. "That's unwashed gym socks."

As they ran through the locker room and weight room and past the swimming pool, Allison revealed her plan. Dani and Binx had to get tennis balls. Max had to get into the school office.

"If everything goes right," Allison said, "I'll see you in the pottery shop."

"And if it doesn't go right, you'll see me in a boiling cauldron," Max replied.

Allison glared at him.

"Okay, okay," Max said. "I'll try to be optimistic. It just isn't easy."

He turned and ran down to the school office. Thank God the door was open. The school had recently installed a new security system with video monitors. Max switched them on and spun through the channels, staring at the small black-and-white monitors in the console. The halls were empty, the cafeteria was empty—there they were! He saw the witches creeping past the rows of metal lockers in the boys locker room. Max quickly turned up the volume.

"I smell boys," Mary was saying. "Sweaty boys."

"Isn't it nice?" Sarah asked.

She's weird, Max thought. He watched as Mary stopped and pulled open a locker. She and Sarah stared in.

" 'Tis for the little ones," she said. "They hang them off these hooks, then close the door." She pointed at the vents. "These holes are for spoilage."

Winifred suddenly bent down between them and grabbed their ears. "And these are for pulling," she snapped as her sisters cried out in pain.

By flipping channels Max was able to follow the witches through the weight room and to the pool. As they came out into the hallway, Max picked up the microphone attached to the school's public-address system. He took a deep breath and turned the volume way up.

"Ho ho ho!" Max's laughter practically shook the building. On the monitor he watched Sarah and Mary jump with fright and clutch Winnie.

"Welcome to high school," Max's voice boomed. "I'm your host, Boris Karloff!"

On the monitor Max could see that Dani had shoved a big cardboard box into position at the top of a nearby stairway.

"Tennis, anyone?" Max asked. That was Dani's cue to spill hundreds of tennis balls down the steps. The witches shrieked in terror and ran down the hall.

"Are we having fun yet?" Max asked. Once again the witches stopped and looked around, trying to figure out where Max's voice was coming from. Max bit his lip, praying they didn't have some special spell that would find him.

"It's time to meet today's contestants," he said through the PA system. "From Salem, Massachusetts, would you please welcome three housewitches and broom jockeys, Sarah, Mary, and Winifred Sanderson. Hey, read any good spell books lately?"

That was Binx's cue to appear. The cat stopped at the far end of the hall.

"Meow there." He wagged his tail at the witches.

"Get him!" Winifred screamed.

Binx took off, and the witches ran after him. Flipping through the channels on the security monitor, Max watched the action. The witches ran into an empty hallway and stopped. Winifred brought her finger to her lips. Max could hear the faint sound of voices speaking in French.

He watched as the witches followed the voices and tiptoed into the pottery shop. Ahead of them was a large walk-in kiln in the shape of an igloo. The witches ducked down and went in. A second later Allison jumped out of her hiding place and slammed the kiln door closed, locking the witches inside.

"All right!" Max jumped up and ran to the pottery shop. By the time he got there, Dani and Binx had also arrived.

"We got 'em!" Dani shouted gleefully. "We nailed 'em!"

As Allison pushed the button to light the kiln, Max and Dani peered through the kiln's small glass window. Suddenly Winifred pressed her face against the window and laughed insanely.

Max and Dani jumped back in fright.

Whooosh! A second later Winifred's face disappeared behind a wall of yellow-and-orange flame. The witches' screams were replaced by the roaring jets of the gas kiln.

They were gone.

7

"WE DID IT!" Dani cried as the kids ran whooping and shouting from the school.

"We nuked 'em!" Max shouted.

"We terminated 'em!" Allison yelled joyfully. She grabbed Dani, and the two of them began to dance around the athletic field under the moonlight.

Max stopped to catch his breath. He couldn't believe they had actually gotten rid of the witches. He felt incredibly relieved. Then he noticed Binx sitting on the grass, staring at the thin column of smoke rising from the school's chimney. Wisps of smoke curled past the full moon.

"You did it, Binx," Max congratulated him. "You stopped them just like you said you would."

"Yeah." Binx nodded, but he didn't seem happy. Max looked across the field at his sister, who was still dancing for joy with Allison.

"Look at that nutjob," he said.

"She's a good kid," Binx said.

"When she's not being a pain," Max said.

"She reminds me of my sister, Emily," Binx said with a sad sigh.

Now Max understood. "You still miss her, don't you?"

Binx nodded.

"Hey," Max said. "You can't keep blaming yourself for what happened three hundred years ago."

Binx turned and looked up at him with yellow eyes. "Take good care of Dani," he said. "You'll never know how precious she is until you lose her."

Max nodded. When it came right down to it, his sister was a pretty good kid—and brave, too. Allison and Dani had stopped dancing and were coming toward them. Binx started to walk away.

"Hey, Binx," Max said. "Where do you think you're going? You lost your family, but you found a new one. You're a Dennison now, buddy."

Binx stopped and turned. "Really?"

"Sure," said Dani. "We've got sunny windows to

lie near. We've got fish in the backyard, and we don't have a dog. Come on, Binx, you're coming home with us."

"Home," Binx repeated. Max had never seen a cat smile before.

They headed home. It was very late now, and the town was quiet. The streets were empty, and the houses were dark. A few jack-o'-lanterns still flickered, but most had burned out.

At his house Max pushed the door open and led the others inside. "Mom! Dad?" he called.

"Guess what?" Dani yelled. "We kept that cat!"

The lights were on, but no one answered. Max looked around and frowned. "Could they still be under that spell?"

"No," Binx said. "When the witches were destroyed, the spell should have been broken."

"Maybe they're still out partying," Dani said.

They got Binx a bowl of milk and went upstairs to Max's room. Dani sat on the floor and petted Binx while he lapped up the milk. Max and Allison sat on Max's bed. Allison yawned and leaned her head on his shoulder. It had been a crazy, scary night, but Max was not displeased with how it was ending.

"That was a great plan," Max said with a smile.

Allison smiled back at him. "Couldn't have done it without you."

They moved their faces close to each other and were about to kiss when Dani cleared her throat. "Ahem, you guys."

Binx finished the bowl of milk and yawned. "That moo juice really hit the spot," he said.

"You're my kitty now," Dani said, petting him. "You'll have milk and tuna fish every day, and you'll only hunt mice for fun."

"You're gonna turn me into one of those fat, useless, contented cats," Binx said, stretching out and closing his eyes.

"I'll always take care of you," Dani said. "And then my children will take care of you and their children and their children after that. Forever and ever . . ."

Dani's words trailed off as she fell asleep. Max realized Allison was asleep, too. His own eyelids were getting heavy. . . .

Max didn't know how long he had slept, but suddenly he felt something stir, and he opened his eyes. It was still dark out. Next to him, Allison was sitting up, awake.

"Hi," he said with a sleepy smile.

"Hi," Allison smiled back, then looked at the radio alarm clock. The red numbers glowed: 4:29. "Oh God," she groaned. "My parents are gonna kill me."

She started to slide off the bed. Max reached out and stopped her.

"You might as well stay a little longer then," he said. He leaned toward her for a kiss. At the last moment Allison turned her head and looked at the black cat sleeping on the floor.

"Poor Binx," she said sadly. "Do you think we could help him? Maybe make him into a boy again?"

"How?" Max asked.

Allison pointed at the spell book lying on the floor near the bed. "The witches used it to put a spell on him," she said. "There might be a way to take the spell off."

"You mean, like a spell remover?" Max asked, intrigued.

"Like maybe if you say it backward or something," Allison said, sliding off the bed and reaching for the book.

"Hey," Max said. "Binx told us not to open it."

"But the witches are dead," Allison said. "I don't see what harm it could do now."

"I don't know," Max said nervously.

"If anything weird happens, we'll slam it shut, okay?" Allison said. She leaned toward Max and pressed her forehead against his. "What do you say?"

Max nodded. If Allison had asked him to do a hand-stand on the roof, he probably would have agreed to do that, too. Allison put the book in her lap. Then she carefully opened it. Neither she nor Max noticed that a strange flamelike black-and-orange force floated out of the open book. They were paying too much attention to the book's reddish brown ink.

"What kind of ink is that?" Max asked.

"It's blood," Allison whispered, sliding her hand into his. She slowly turned the stiff, warped pages. "Here's something! 'Only a circle of salt can protect thy victims from thy power.' "

"I'm not sure that's going to help Binx," Max whispered.

Suddenly a black paw slammed the book shut, and Binx jumped on top of it. Startled, Max and Allison sat up straight.

"I told you not to open it!" Binx hissed angrily at them.

"We were just trying to help you," Allison explained.

"Well, don't," Binx snapped. "Nothing good can come from this book."

Allison shrugged and glanced again at the radio alarm clock. "I better get home," she said.

"Wait," Max said, not wanting her to go. "I can't let you walk home alone at this time of night, but I can't leave Dani alone, either. I mean, the witches are gone, but Billy the Zombie may still be out there somewhere."

"We could leave a circle of salt around Dani," Allison said. "Then she'd be protected while you walked me home."

Max liked that idea. They got Dani into Max's bed and pulled the covers up over her. Max took his pocketknife out of his drawer and went downstairs into the kitchen with Allison. He found a box of salt in the pantry and handed it to Allison, who read the label.

"Yup, it says right here, 'Pour a circle of salt to protect from zombies, witches, and old boyfriends.' "

"What about *new* boyfriends?" Max asked, leaning toward her for a kiss. Once again Allison turned away.

"Did you hear something?" she whispered.

"No." Max wondered if Allison kept turning away on purpose.

"I'm sure I heard something," Allison said. "I think it came from upstairs."

Moments later they stepped back into Max's bedroom. Dani was still sleeping peacefully under the blankets. Everything looked okay.

"Max!" Allison grabbed his arm. "The spell book is gone!"

She was right. They'd left it on the bed, and now it wasn't there. Max quickly looked around. Binx was nowhere in sight.

"Where's Binx?" he asked.

"He's gone, too," Allison said, sounding scared. "Max, this is weird."

Max turned back to the bed. "Dani, wake up," he said, pulling the covers back.

But Dani wasn't there.

Sarah was!

"Trick or treat," Sarah said with a wink.

"Ahhhhhh!" Max and Allison jumped back and screamed. The door of the closet flew open, and Winifred stepped out with an evil grin on her face and the spell book in her hands. Mary was right behind her, holding Dani tightly and carrying a sack with an angry meowing cat inside.

"Looking for this?" Winifred asked, holding the spell book up. She and her sisters howled with laughter. Not knowing what else to do, Max suddenly charged her, but Winifred opened the book in his face, and a surge of evil green power knocked him backward.

Crunch! Max smashed into the wall and slid to the floor, dazed.

"Max!" Allison screamed and ran to him. Winifred shrieked with wicked laughter and followed. Allison quickly spilled a circle of salt on the floor around herself and Max.

"Salt!" Winifred screeched. "Such a clever little witch. But it will not save thy friends! Come, Sisters, we must hurry! The candle's magic will soon be spent. Dawn approaches! We have children's lives to consume."

Winifred raised her hands to the ceiling.

Craaaack! She blew a hole straight through the

roof. Holding the spell book tightly, she picked up an old straw broom and flew off. Sarah mounted a dust mop and followed with Binx. Mary brought up the rear, holding Dani and riding a vacuum cleaner.

"*Max!*" Dani screamed as Mary took off into the sky. "*Help meeeeee!*"

8

ALLISON RAN TO THE WINDOW and pulled it open. She watched as the witches flew off, silhouetted by the full moon.

Her eyes went wide. She turned and shook Max's shoulder. "Max . . . Max!"

"Wha . . . ?" Max slowly came out of his daze. "Dani? Where's Dani?"

"They took her," Allison said.

"What?" Max rose unsteadily to his feet. "I gotta get her!" He staggered a few feet and then fell.

"Take it easy, Max," Allison said.

"But they're going to steal her life, and it's all my

fault," Max moaned unhappily. "I had to go and light that stupid candle."

Suddenly the sound of chanting floated through the gaping hole in the ceiling.

"It's Sarah!" Allison gasped, pulling open the window. "She's singing to the children!"

Max staggered to the window. Outside, dozens of kids in pajamas were wandering up the street like zombies.

"Hey, you guys!" Max cupped his hands around his mouth and shouted, "Don't listen to her!"

"It's no use," Allison said. "They ate the candy. They're under the spell."

Max turned from the window and let his hands fall helplessly to his sides. "They've already got Dani, and more kids are on the way. We can't make the sun come up any faster. I mean, we really need a miracle."

Allison nodded and stared out the open window. Then she turned to him. "Max, can you drive?"

Max didn't know why she was asking nor how to answer. The last thing he wanted to admit was that he couldn't drive. Finally, he just said, "Hey, I'm from California."

"Great," Allison said, heading out of the room. "I noticed the car keys on a hook in the kitchen. Let's go."

The next thing Max knew, Allison was going down

the stairs. By the time he caught up to her, she was already unlocking the passenger door of his parents' station wagon. She tossed the keys over the roof to Max. "Let's go," she said.

Max got behind the wheel and stuck the key in the ignition. The truth was, he didn't know how to drive. But how hard could it be? It had to be pretty simple, considering how many adults did it.

Max turned the ignition key. Nothing happened.

"It won't start," he said.

"Put it in neutral," Allison said.

"Right." Max slid the gear lever into neutral and turned the key again. This time the engine roared to life.

"Lights," Allison said.

"Sure." Max looked around for the light switch. Finally, Allison leaned over and turned them on.

"We're a good team," she said with a wink.

"Yeah," Max said, relieved that she didn't make fun of him. He shifted into reverse. The car bucked and wouldn't back up.

"Parking brake," Allison said.

"Right." Max reached down and released the parking brake.

When he looked back up, Allison was staring at him. "You sure you can drive?"

"No problem," Max said.

"Buckle up," Allison said, pulling the seat belt across her chest.

Max backed the car slowly down the driveway and out into the street. He started to navigate through the crowd of zombielike kids drifting up the road toward the Sanderson house. As long as he didn't get pulled over by the cops, he figured he'd be fine.

A little while later Max crept slowly across the grass to the Sanderson house. Several dozen glassy-eyed kids surrounded the house, waiting to be summoned inside. Max slid past them and stared in through the window. He couldn't believe what he saw. Those two jerks Jay and Ernie were trapped in a cage hanging from a roof beam. They were barefoot, and Mary was pressing candy toward them. A big pile of empty candy wrappers lay on the floor beneath the cage.

"Stuff yourselves!" Mary said merrily.

"No more candy!" Jay begged.

"I'm gonna barf!" Ernie groaned.

Across the room, near the fireplace, Dani was tied to a chair. Winifred stood over a cauldron of bubbling greenish goo, studying her spell book.

"Soon the lives of all thy little friends will be mine," the witch cackled. "And I will be young and beautiful again forever!"

"It doesn't matter how young or old you are," Dani

shot back defiantly. "You sold your soul. You're the ugliest thing that's ever lived, and you know it."

Max watched, petrified. He knew his little sister had a lot of guts, but she was crazy to aggravate a witch as powerful as Winifred.

Winifred glared at Dani, who defiantly glared right back.

"Can you do this?" Winifred yelled, and viciously bit off a piece of her own tongue, spitting it into the pot. The goo turned purple and began to hiss and boil, giving off a menacing curl of purple vapor.

"I wouldn't even if I could," Dani said.

"You die first," Winifred said with a sinister chuckle as she dipped a ladle into the cauldron.

Across the room a sack kicked and jerked. Through the window, Max heard Binx shout, "Don't drink it, Dani!"

Dani clamped her mouth shut. Winifred turned to her sisters.

"Pry her mouth open," she ordered.

Do something! Max told himself, but it felt as if his legs were paralyzed with fear. Inside the room Mary tried to force Dani's mouth open, but Dani bit her instead. Sarah stepped up next, but Dani kicked her in the shin. Now Winifred pointed her clawlike fingernails at Max's sister.

Max knew Dani didn't have a chance.

He had to do something . . . now! Remember what

happened to Binx, he thought. He didn't act in time, and he lost Emily.

Winifred's hands were only inches from Dani.

Max yanked open the door and burst into the room.

"Prepare to die . . . again!" he shouted.

The witches spun around and gave him puzzled looks. Winifred smiled.

"Fool!" she shouted. "You have no powers."

"Maybe not," Max said. "But there's a power even greater than your magic. It's called knowledge. And I know something that you don't."

"What is that?" Winifred smirked.

"Daylight savings time!" Max shouted.

Suddenly a bird began to sing outside, and the rosy light of dawn began to shine through the windows.

"The sun!" Sarah screamed.

"We're dust!" Mary cried. They rushed to Winifred and clung to her. "Save us, Winnie! Save us!"

In the confusion Max took out his pocketknife and cut the ropes holding Dani, then dumped the boiling cauldron over. He grabbed the sack containing Binx.

"Hey, Hollywood, help us out of here!" Ernie cried from the cage.

Max bent down, picked up his cross-trainers, and waved at the caged jerks. "Tubular, dudes!" He headed for the door, then realized Dani was just standing there.

"Come on, Dani, let's go!" he shouted.

"Wait," Dani said. "I want to see them turn to dust."

Max grabbed her and dragged her toward the door.

"No, wait!" Dani yelled. "I really want to see . . . huh?"

Outside it was still dark. Allison was standing in the shadows, whistling like a bird. The family station wagon was parked nearby, with red T-shirts covering its headlights to simulate the dawn.

As they ran toward the car, they could hear Winifred shriek, "Let go of me, you fools! The sun rises in the east. That light is coming from the west!"

Max and the others reached the car and jumped in.

"Head for the graveyard!" Binx gasped. "It's our only chance."

Max did a quick U-turn and started to drive back down the hill, once again weaving in and out of the sleepwalking children.

"Wow," Dani gasped from the front seat. "It's a zombie pajama party!"

They got past the kids and picked up speed. Allison turned and looked out the back window.

"Are they following us?" Max asked.

"No," Allison said.

An instant later Max saw why. Riding the broom, dust mop, and vacuum cleaner, the witches were headed straight toward them!

Dani and Allison screamed and ducked under the dashboard, but Max clenched his teeth and held the wheel steady. At the last instant the witches veered away.

"Great driving, Bro!" Dani yelled.

Max had called the witches' bluff, but he knew they'd be back. He looked out the side window. Winifred raced up beside him.

"Pull over!" she shouted. "Let me see your driver's permit!"

Max swerved the car toward her. Winifred screamed as her broom veered off. *Thwomp!* She crashed into a tree.

"Yeah, Max!" Everyone in the car cheered.

A few minutes later the station wagon pulled up to the old graveyard, and everyone scrambled out. Max grabbed a baseball bat from the back and took the lead. As he ran through the trees, one of them suddenly moved.

Thunk! Max smashed into it and fell to the ground. The baseball bat went flying. He looked up and gasped. It wasn't a tree at all. Standing over him was Billy Butcherson! Max quickly reached for his pocketknife. But before he could get it open, Billy reached down and grabbed it.

Click! The blade snapped open. Billy stood above Max with the knife in his hand.

9

MAX WAS SURE he was done for. Billy raised the knife . . . and cut the stitches across his mouth. To Max's amazement the zombie breathed a sigh of relief. Dust, moths, and a horrible stench came out of his mouth.

"It's about time," Billy sighed. He stared down at Max, who still cowered fearfully on the ground. "Hey, I'm not chasing you. I hate those witches, too. Let me help you."

"You're a *good* zombie?" Dani asked in amazement as she ran up.

"As good as a zombie can be," Billy replied.

"Then come on!" Max shouted, jumping to his feet

and grabbing the bat. They ran through the graveyard until they came to an open space between the graves.

"Okay," Max shouted. "This is where we'll make our stand."

"Are you sure?" Allison asked.

"No, but I don't think we have a lot of choices," Max replied.

He held his bat ready. Allison took out the box of salt. Binx hopped up on Emily's gravestone and watched the sky for the witches. Billy led Dani to his grave.

"You'll be safe in here," he said.

"Thanks, Billy," Dani said, and got into the grave.

"Here they come!" Binx shouted.

Max looked up and saw the three witches come screaming out of the moonlit sky like kamikaze pilots. Holding the baseball bat tightly, he ducked behind a tall headstone. As Winifred zoomed toward him on her straw broom, he jumped out and took a swing.

"Ooof!" The next thing Max knew, he was lying on his back. Hovering in the air above him, Winifred cackled. She had the bat in her hand!

Sarah flew at Allison, who threw salt in her face.

"Aaaiiieeeee!" the pretty blond witch screamed as the salt stung her.

Straddling her vacuum cleaner, Mary flew at Dani. Billy stood in her way.

Thwackkk! Mary kicked Billy's head off. It rolled

away, and Billy fell to his hands and knees to search for it. Dani jumped out of the grave and grabbed Billy's head.

"Here you go, Billy." She handed it to him.

"Hey, thanks," Billy said.

The witches hovered in the air. Max wondered what they'd try next. It wasn't long before he had the answer. Winifred grabbed the plug of the vacuum cleaner Mary was riding. The air around them crackled as the red-haired witch filled the machine with electrical current.

Vaaarrroooommm! The supercharged vacuum cleaner roared like a motorcycle and started to suck with incredible power. Max felt it tug on his hair and clothes. All around him sticks and leaves were being sucked into the air.

"Max!" Dani screamed.

Max and Allison spun around. Mary had positioned the vacuum right over Dani, and it was sucking her into the air.

"Grab her!" Max shouted.

Billy lurched toward her, but it was too late. Dani was sucked up in the air and into Winifred's clutches.

"Dani!" Max cried desperately. But Winifred held his sister tightly. Grasping Dani's hand in hers, the witch waved it like a doll's.

"Bye-bye, big brother!" she cackled, hovering just

above the trees. Max watched in horror as Winifred took out a vial and opened it with her teeth.

"It must be the potion!" Allison gasped. "The one that steals children's lives."

"Max!" Dani screamed again. But there was nothing Max could do except watch helplessly from below as Winifred pressed the vial toward his sister's lips.

With a sudden pantherlike yowl, Binx leapt from a tall branch and knocked the vial out of Winifred's hand. It plummeted downward, but Max caught it before it could crash to the ground.

"Give me that vial, or your sister dies!" Winifred screamed as she threw Binx to the ground, where he lay motionless.

"Let her go!" Max shouted back, holding the vial aloft. "Or I'll smash it—and it's the last vial you've got!"

Winifred closed her hands around Dani's throat as if to strangle her. "What have I got to lose?" she asked.

Max realized she was right. If she couldn't have Dani *and* the potion, she'd die. So why not take Dani with her? It was a standoff. Max searched desperately through his mind for a way to save his sister. He had to come up with something . . . anything!

Wait!

There was a way . . . the only way. Max pressed the vial to his lips.

"Max, don't!" Allison cried.

It was too late. Max tilted the vial back and let the bitter potion drain into his mouth. It burned his throat and made his stomach churn wildly.

"Let Dani go," he shouted up at the witches. "You can have me instead."

Just as Max had hoped, Winifred dropped down and let go of Dani. The witch then reached for him, and Max allowed her to pick him up. His body felt hot, as if he had a fever. He felt himself begin to glow with the light of his life-force.

"What a fool," Winifred mumbled in disgust. "To give up thy life for thy sister."

She burst into laughter. Max knew this was his only chance. He pulled his arm free and punched her in the face.

"*Aaaaahhhh!*" They both tumbled off the broom and fell to the graveyard below.

"*Winnie!*" her sisters shrieked as Winifred fell to the hallowed earth. Max hit the ground hard and lay there stunned while his life-force glowed around him.

Everyone stared at Winifred, waiting for something terrible to happen. But nothing did. Max turned and looked helplessly at Allison. Was the legend wrong?

Winifred rose to her feet and aimed her long, pointed fingernails at Max. "Why, you little . . ."

She tried to take a step toward him, but her feet

wouldn't move. They seemed frozen to the ground. Suddenly strange protrusions started to grow out of her back.

"Oh no! . . . No!" she screamed.

"Max, look!" Allison yelled, pointing to the east. Max turned and saw a pink glow. The sun was coming up! In the air above them, Mary and Sarah also saw it.

"If I am not mistaken, Sister," Mary said, "that bright object over there is the . . . uh oh."

The first rays of dawn broke through the trees and fell on Mary and Sarah. Max and the others gasped as they instantly turned to dust.

Clunk! The dust mop and vacuum cleaner crashed to the graveyard ground.

"NOOOOOOOOOO!" Winifred raised her arms to her face and tried to shield herself. But as the light hit her, her hands involuntarily clasped before her and the growths from her back spread out like wings. Max and the others stared in amazement as she became gray and faceless like the tombstones around her.

"She turned into an angel!" Dani gasped.

"An angel of stone," Allison said in wonder.

Still lying on the ground, Max felt his glowing life-force start to seep back into his body. Dani and Allison ran to him.

"Max!" Allison cried. "Are you all right?"

"I think so." Max got up slowly.

"Oh, Max, you saved my life," Dani said, throwing her arms around his neck. For the first time in a long time he didn't mind her doing that.

"I'm your brother," Max said with a grin. "It's my job."

Dani hugged him. "I love you, jerkface."

Over Dani's shoulder, Max's eyes met Allison's. She was smiling, and her eyes were filled with admiration.

"Hey, guys." They turned and saw Billy the Zombie standing up in his grave, waving at them.

"See you around," he said with a yawn, then flopped into his grave. A big cloud of dust rose.

"Where's Binx?" Dani asked.

"There!" Allison pointed to the spot where the black cat still lay. She bent down and nudged him, but Binx didn't move.

"I'm afraid he's really gone this time," Allison said sadly.

"No, he *can't* die, remember?" Dani said, kneeling next to him. "He's supposed to live forever. Come on, Binx, wake up."

She petted the cat, but he didn't stir.

"Please, Binx?" Dani started to cry. "Please don't die now."

The cat still didn't move. Dani looked up at Allison with tear-streaked eyes. "But I thought he couldn't die!"

"The witches are gone for good," Allison said sadly. "Their evil spells are all broken."

"Look!" Max said. A few feet away from them the transparent figure of a boy appeared. He was dressed in a colonial nightshirt and sleeping cap.

"Thackery Binx, is that you?" Dani asked, wide-eyed.

The boy nodded and held out his hands to her. Dani reached forward, and their fingertips touched. A tear fell out of her eye.

"Don't be sad for me, Dani," Thackery said. "You freed me. I'm happy now. This is where I'm meant to be."

"But I'll miss you," Dani said with a sniff.

"Don't worry, I'll always be with you," Thackery said. He turned to Allison and Max. "Thanks for lighting the candle, Max."

"Thackery! Thackery Binx!" a voice cried. Max and the others turned and saw the transparent form of a young girl waving from across the graveyard.

"Coming, Em!" Thackery called back.

"Hurry!" the girl called impatiently. "Father is furious!"

Thackery nodded and turned to the others. "Nothing changes," he said with a smile and a shrug, then started toward her.

"What took thee so long?" Emily Binx asked in a huff. A moment later they ran off and vanished.

"Look over there." Allison pointed toward the street that led past the graveyard. Dozens of sleepy-faced, bewildered-looking kids were walking quickly toward town.

Dani was still wiping the tears out of her eyes when she felt something rub against her leg. "Hey!" she cried, bending down and picking up the black cat. "Binx, can you talk?"

The cat just meowed.

"That's okay. Meowing is good." Dani hugged the cat to her chest and turned to Allison and Max. "I guess he still had one life left."

Max and Allison turned and smiled at each other. Max pulled her close. He almost expected her to turn her head away at the last moment, but this time she didn't. They shared a soft, lingering kiss.

"So, did I make a believer out of you?" Allison asked, pulling back and smiling at him.

"Yeah, you did." Max smiled back.

"I'm glad." Allison started to lean toward him for another kiss.

"Excuse me, you two," Dani said. "Can we go home now, please?"

"Sure." Max was so happy, he lifted Dani up so she could ride on his shoulders.

"You shouldn't have saved my life," Dani told him as she held on to his head. "Because now I'm going to bug you forever."

"I know," Max said.

And he couldn't help but smile.